Chapter 1

As I sat staring out of the car window I counted the trees   ,, or at least I was trying to count the trees, I could only make it to 2_ and even then I wasn't sure if that was the correct number or not as the faster the car went the blurrier the trees became, one merged into another and I would close my eyes for a second and try to re-focus before starting the whole process again. This continued throughout my journey as it was a much easier use of my time than thinking! You see if I had allowed myself to think, then I might not like what I think about, I didn't want to relive the awfulness of the situation I found myself in, I didn't want to think, I didn't want to cry, I didn't want to know or understand what had happened, I certainly didn't want my emotions taking over my body and leaving me like a weak, fragile little girl with no control! So I just kept on counting the hazy trees as they rushed past the window of the black BMW that was carrying me to my unknown future.

It was early August time 1990 and the sun was blaring down on all who ventured into it. I didn't realise how hot it actually was thanks to the BMWs cool air nipping at my bare knees, it was actually making me feel a little shivery but I wouldn't dare say this, I wouldn't dare say anything, I hadn't spoken a word since the incident and I wasn't going to start now! Had I told people what I thought had happened they would have me thrown in the loony bin for sure, my mum had always said I had a vivid imagination, but I'm almost certain I didn't imagine this. For now I would keep my thoughts and opinions to myself and just continue to be mute, I wondered to myself if I would ever speak again, maybe I would forget how to, I don't think I wanted to lose my voice forever, just for now, just until I could make sense of what had happened, I just hoped it wouldn't take too long.

I glanced over at my sister Sammi who was also staring out of the window, I wondered if she too was trying to count the trees, I could see part of her reflection in the glass, her eyes looked sad and old, she had our mums eyes, always looking too tired to even be open, constantly filled with worry about things I had no knowledge of, at the time I just saw sadness and tiredness but now looking back and remembering that look I can see it was a look of grief and exhaustion, I couldn't understand why Sammi looked so sad, I mean I was sad that our mother had died but not quite as sad as Sammi, maybe she knew more than I did, she was older after all, only by 2 years though! can you have that much more wisdom with only 2 years of learning? I didn't think so. Sammi always thought she was so much smarter than me just because she had 2 years on me! She was wrong though, I knew things that she could never understand, at least I thought I did. I found my mind wandering back to the previous night and I gripped Emily closer to my chest, Emily was my ragdoll, she wasn't much to look at, a soft knitted doll in a pink polka dot dress, her hair was made from thick yellow wool and had 2 shabby pigtails that id proudly done myself 3 days earlier in an effort to make her look better. I was given Emily for my 8ᵗʰ birthday 6 months earlier off Sammi, our mum had used all of her money on bills and alcohol so I knew not to expect anything off her, it had been like that for a couple of years since our dad left. Mum had always made sure we had a roof over our head and a little food in our stomachs so we were thankful and grateful for that, at least she had stuck around unlike our dad! First sign of hard work and he had vanished. I had always felt responsible for him abandoning us, I heard them arguing the night before he left, he told mum she had to take me to see a doctor but she refused, I didn't know I was sick, I certainly didn't feel sick. My dad never understood me and my imagination, sometimes it was like he didn't want to be in the same room as me, sometimes I think my mum and Sammi would have been better off if it was me who disappeared instead of our dad, maybe they would have been happier, a proper family who got presents on their birthdays and laughed with each other and enjoyed spending time together, a nice normal family without the weird kid! I hugged Emily tighter and remembered when Sammi had given her to me, she had earned a couple of pound off the neighbours for shovelling there garden pathways in January to get rid of the snow that had bombarded us that winter, there wasn't much a 10 year old could do to earn money but she was good at snow shovelling. Sammi saved the money she had made and went to a flea market near where we lived, she was so proud when she handed me my birthday gift. Emily was tatty and clearly well loved, Sammi told me Emily was magical, she could protect me, if I ever felt scared or threatened all I had to do was squeeze Emily and tell her why and she would make me feel better, I instantly loved Emily, I didn't care that she wasn't brand new or that she was so tatty looking, she would be my new best friend and confidant, at least whilst Sammi was away. She was going to uncle Phil's for the weekend, she would go there once a month ever since aunt Bella died, mum had said he just needs a woman's touch , a hand with laundry and washing up, a bit of company now and then, someone to talk to and watch a movie with, it didn't seem like such a bad job, and he paid mum too. This all seemed like chores we had at home anyways so at least at uncle Phil's Sammi could chill and watch a movie too. I was quite envious to be honest, Sammi was escaping our miserable home for a couple of days, it wasn't a bad home, it was just so depressing since dad left, he didn't even leave a note, he never said goodbye, that's when mums drinking got worse! we didn't have much money as it was so her spending half of it on vodka every week didn't help. she had quit her job due to depression and now we lived on benefits, it was quite normal back then in our neighbourhood to grow up on government handouts so I don't know why I felt so ashamed, when mum and dad worked for their money I did feel like I was a little better than anyone else, I didn't have to have free school meals, that was the giveaway that let everyone know you came from a benefit family. Although embarrassing it was a perfectly normal way of life back in our little city of Salford homeland, but now my sister was getting to escape for the weekend and she didn't even seem happy about it, I Couldn't wait till my mum thought I was old enough to go help out our uncle with chores, I daydreamed frequently about maybe going with Sammi, we could get the chores done quick as a flash if we did them together and then we would have all weekend to chill out with uncle Phil.

I looked into Sammi's sad eyes when she had given me Emily, she told me that I may need Emily's protection one day if she wasn't there to protect me, I never understood why she wouldn't be there, what did she mean? But I never questioned it, I was just so happy to have a birthday gift off my sister.

Chapter 2

The black BMW slowly pulled to a stop, I could see a large house with 2 cars in the driveway. Sammi turned and looked at me for a second, she took hold of my hand and said *"we've got this Lucy"*, with her warm hand gripping mine I already felt better, it had always been Sammi and Lucy against the world (and Emily of course) moving onto the next chapter of my life with my sister by my side felt achievable.

Our social worker got out of the car and opened the back door *"come on girls, let's go meet your new foster family"*. The thought of a new family scared me a little, what if something bad happened here? Something bad always seems to happen wherever we go, I hoped they would be a nice family, in my head I didn't believe bad things could happen to nice people, only bad people deserved the bad things that would happen to them, it was a very simple way of thinking and one I truly believed.

"hello, you must be Sammi and Lucy" a funny looking lady was standing in the doorway trying to engage us in conversation, she was a plump woman with short curly brown hair, she had a mole on her chin that had a couple of wispy white hairs growing from it, *"I'm Carol, and this is my husband Ed, its lovely to meet you both"* , a tall skinny man stood by her side, he wore beige shorts that showed the whole world his knobbly knees, and he had brown sandals on with white sports socks. The pair were nothing like our mum and dad, mum had been quite pretty once before the alcohol consumed her, and our dad was a big butch bloke, one you wouldn't mess with, these pair looked fresh out of a story book I remembered reading about a witch and a weasel, I reminded myself not to be so judgemental right away, how they looked wasn't important. Sammi let go of my hand and went to greet them, I didn't like that she let go of my hand, she had another one! But I suppose at least this way I wasn't being tugged along to pass pleasantries.

Our social worker Amanda took us inside and got us settled with some juice and biscuits, Amanda was a nice lady, I felt for sure that nothing bad would ever happen to her. She was tall and had a pretty face, her smile made me feel instantly at ease, she liked to joke with us as well, always trying to make us laugh, I often laughed at her silly jokes but Sammi never felt like laughing anymore, not since mum died. I understood that it was sad when someone died but it had been almost a day now, you can't not laugh or smile for an entire day, I couldn't figure out if it was Sammi that was the strange one or me! is it wrong to smile and be a little happy even though your mums just died? Amanda had long red hair, it wasn't straight or curly, it was in between, when id first met her about a year ago I remember thinking she looked like a fairy tale princess, but the more time I spent with her the more I realised that princesses don't talk the way she talks, she would occasionally use a swear word in front of us by accident and then swear when apologising for swearing, I didn't mind though, she was funny, and even though she swore it didn't make her bad, me and Emily liked her even if she wasn't a princess.

Amanda said her goodbyes and assured us we would be fine here with the Bowlers, Carol and Ed Bowler, maybe they would be nice people and nothing bad would happen, only time would tell.

The Bowlers left us to settle into our room, it was a nice pink and blue room, there were bunk beds in the corner, 2 wardrobes and 2 sets of draws. Sammi claimed the top bunk because she was the eldest, I didn't mind though, I was just glad we got to share a room, id hated the thought of being separated from my sister, my protector, ever since my first and only weekend away at uncle Phil's about 6 months ago.

I had been so happy that I was finally considered mature enough to do uncle Phil's chores, Sammi had cried when she realised I was going instead of her, petty jealousy I thought, I couldn't understand why she was being like that, she had been going for months now so it was only fare I got a turn. As I waved goodbye to mum, Sammi had grabbed hold of me tightly, she told me to be brave, she told me she wished it was her going and she was so sorry that it was my turn, she pressed Emily into my chest, just keep squeezing Emily ok! and when you come home I will be waiting for you. I couldn't work out what was wrong with Sammi, she didn't seem jealous, it felt more like fear that was coming from her, I just didn't know why, maybe she was just scared of being with mum on her own all weekend, silly Sammi, I had thought, mum wasn't scary, she would just drink until she passed out and then it was our job to make sure she hadn't fell asleep with a lit cigarette in her hand, nothing that scary at all. I waved goodbye, put my mind at ease over Sammi and was happily off for a good weekend with uncle Phil.

"Tea time" Carol bellowed upstairs, as Sammi and I walked into the dining room we noticed there was a couple of kids waiting patiently. *"I'm Brian and this is my sister Brittany"*, Brian and Brittany looked very similar, both had dark hair and pokey noses, both were skinny and bothersome looking, another boy walked into the room, he looked nervous and fearful, Brian and Brittany whispered to each other and sniggered, as the boy went to sit down Brian booted his chair from under him and he fell to the floor, the boy quickly stood up as Brian and Brittany laughed like a pair of hyenas. The Bowlers questioned what had just happened but the boy said nothing, Brian politely told them that Michael was messing about with his chair and fell over, the Bowlers happily accepted this as an explanation and scolded Michael for messing around at the dining table. I couldn't believe how Michael didn't say anything, why didn't he

defend himself? why didn't he tell them what had really happened? I wanted to scream at Brian and tell the Bowlers what really happened but I couldn't risk opening my mouth, I never knew what would come out of it, I just gripped Emily hard as I could and angrily glared at Brian instead.

After tea we were allowed to watch television in the living room for an hour before going to our rooms, I didn't feel much like spending time with Brian so I followed Sammi up to our room instead, Sammi never felt like socialising anymore, not for a long time, ever since she had started going to uncle Phil's house. Going there had changed her, made her grow up more I think.

As we drove away from my house uncle Phil was telling me how pleased he was that I was going to be his "pretend wife" for the weekend, I laughed at the thought of playing house with him. I remember thinking how bad his car smelt, like stale cigarettes and beer, it was a dirty car, a white Lada, although with the amount of dirt it was covered in it looked more greyish, the inside was dirty too, covered in dust and other dirt from his job as a builder, it clearly hadn't had a good clean for a long time, maybe my job this weekend would be to clean the car, I wouldn't mind that, I may need a step ladder to reach the top but it could be fun. It was a 30 minute car ride to his house, "nearly there babe" he said as he grabbed my knee, he began rubbing his hand along the edge of my skirt as he told me how much he was looking forward to this. He lived on a council estate like us but it looked cleaner and the air was fresher, our house was a terraced with just a small back yard, uncle Phil's house was a semi-detached with a driveway he had built himself and a large back garden which was overgrown, "welcome to your new weekend home", I smiled and jumped out of the car eager to see what my weekend would bring.

Sammi climbed onto the top bunk, *"i saw the way you scowled at Brian, you have to keep them feelings under control Luce, these are nice people, they don't deserve bad stuff okay?"* I saw the worried look on her face and I nodded in agreement, Sammi said she was tired and we should just go to sleep and maybe tomorrow would be a better day, I climbed into my bed and held Emily tightly, I told her all my worries from the day in silence, I believed she could hear my thoughts, I didn't really need to speak my fears, Emily had always protected me since the day I got her, I felt comfort when I confessed my feelings to her, I knew that somehow she *would* magically sort them out for me just like she always did.

Chapter 3

Uncle Phil lived in what my mum would describe as a pigsty, I realised I had my work cut out for me this weekend, it took me 2 hours to clean the kitchen, uncle Phil had been sat drinking beer and watching the football on the tv, I told him I was finished in there so he came to inspect, as I eagerly awaited my well earned praise I notice his face changed, he grabbed my hair tightly and yanked me to the floor where I had missed some sticky stuff, uncle Phil yelled at me and said if it wasn't clean in 10 minutes I would have to lick it clean! He left the room and I lay where he left me wondering what the hell had just happened!, even in my mums drunken state she had never acted that way towards me. I wiped away my tears and quickly started scrubbing the floor with a scouring pad. When uncle Phil came back into the kitchen I was terrified id missed something else, he took my hands and told me what a good job I'd done, he smiled kindly at me and said he shouldn't of lost his temper like that and he was sorry. I felt a bit more at ease and accepted it for what it was, just a silly misunderstanding. Because I'd done such a good job he said we could have a chippy tea, I hadn't had chippy for ages, I was so excited. After tea uncle Phil went for a bath so I got to relax and watch tv for a bit on my own, shortly after he yelled down at me to get my bath, said his wife had to be clean. I got my pyjamas ready and ran into the bathroom but was shocked to see him still laying in the tub, I giggled and told him he was silly, how could I have a bath if he was still in it. "this is what a wife does Lucy, she shares a bath with her husband, helps him wash the bits he can't reach and then the husband does the same for his wife, and it's also a way of saving water". I didn't feel comfortable getting in the tub naked with my naked uncle!, it didn't feel right but he insisted, he passed me the sponge and told me to wash his back, then I had to wash his stomach, he told me what a great job I was doing, gave me the attention I craved, he took my hands and rubbed soap into them until they lathered, "don't need a sponge for this body part lucy" he put my hands on his penis and told me to wash it clean, I didn't like it, not one bit, we had a lesson at school about good touch bad touch and this felt so bad. As I lathered his penis with soap he began rubbing his soapy hands over my body, said he was cleaning me as I cleaned him, he had to get to all the hard to reach places, he smoothed his hand between my legs and I jerked backwards, "its ok lucy, this is just what husbands and wife's do, you want to be a good wife don't you" he slipped a finger inside of me and it hurt, he told me I was to just ignore what he was doing and concentrate on cleaning his penis, surely it was clean by now! I felt the tears pricking my eyes and before I knew it I was sobbing uncontrollably,

Uncle Phil lost his temper again and slapped me across my face, I was stunned, caught off guard again! he ordered me out of the tub, told me I was too much of a baby to be his wife if I acted like this, he told me to get into bed and think about if I was a grown up or not, he said we could try again tomorrow night but if I didn't please him like a wife should then he would just have to go back to having Sammi stay over.

I lay in my bed at uncle Phil's house and cried into Emily's soft comforting knitted body. Everything had felt so wrong, I felt dirty and like id failed at my one chance, I didn't want to do it again tomorrow (I confided to Emily), Maybe I was just too young to be his pretend wife, if Sammi was so good at it she could just keep doing it. I remembered how Sammi's behaviour had changed since she had been going to uncle Phil's house, how she never wanted to socialise anymore, she seemed lost in her own head most of the time, the only emotion she ever shown was when she wanted to protect me. Maybe I'd got it wrong all this time, I don't think Sammi liked coming here at all, did uncle Phil make her do this every weekend? I sobbed to Emily that I thought uncle Phil was a bad man, "bad people deserve bad things Emily", I slowly cried myself to sleep thinking of the bad things that should happen" I know you will protect me Emily, Sammi told me so".

Chapter 4

Waking up in the bowler house felt weird, Sammi was nowhere to be found, I looked all over, even stuck my head in a room we hadn't been shown, *" you okay Lucy"* Carol was in that room, *"this is a private room lucy, no children are allowed in here, it's the grownups office"* she ushered me out of the room and into the kitchen, she placed an assortment of cereals on the table for me to choose from, my eyes still awkwardly searching for Sammi. *"are you wondering where Sammi is love, she's gone shopping with Ed, they won't be long, she's an early bird like him she is"* I breathed a sigh of relief, she hadn't abandoned me, she was just shopping. As I tucked into a bowl of cornflakes Carol sat beside me, *"I hear that you can speak, you just choose not to, is that right?"* I nodded. Carol looked at me with sadness in her eyes, *"well when you're ready my lovely, I'm here, no pressure, just in your own time"* , she seemed sincere, and I wanted to speak to her and tell her all my thoughts and fears but I just couldn't risk it, she will definitely think I'm bonkers if I tell her my dolls magic and I think she punishes bad people, I had no choice but to keep my mouth firmly closed.

"when I woke that next morning at uncle Phil's house it felt different, it had a strange kind of silence screaming at me through the walls, "uncle Phil?" I shouted as I walked downstairs, I couldn't see him anywhere, I noticed the clock, it was 11:30, I never slept this late, I can't imagine uncle Phil ever does either. I went into the kitchen and helped myself to cereal, I'm sure he won't mind, its nearly lunch time after all. Whilst I ate my cereal I had decided I was going to tell uncle Phil I didn't feel well and wanted to go home, we could try me being his pretend wife another time, I certainly didn't want to try it again tonight so I had to go home. As time passed by I started to tidy up the living room, "this will put him in a good mood" I thought to myself. I looked at the clock, it was nearly 1:00 in the afternoon, I grew more curious as to where he could be, I went up to his bedroom to check if he was sleeping but there was no sign of him, it didn't even look as though his bed had been slept in. I went back into my room and sat on the bed clutching Emily, I didn't like being all alone, I just wanted to go home now, maybe he had left me by myself to punish me for not being a good wife to him last night, I hugged Emily closer to my chest, I noticed the ends of her hair were wet, "what have you been up to Emily" I thought maybe I had spilled a drink in my sleep or maybe I sat her too close to my cereal earlier, I stared at Emily looking for answers but she didn't speak to me, she just looked happy with herself as she always did with her big smiley mouth made from red wool. I grabbed my toothbrush and headed to the bathroom, I was determined that when uncle Phil got home I would be ready to go. The floor boards creaked as I walked along the hallway, the house felt older and less inviting as it did yesterday, the wallpaper was peeling down the wall and the banister rail needed a coat of paint, I heard a creak behind me and suddenly became overwhelmed with a sense of dread, I turned to look but there was no one there, I shook off the feeling and opened the bathroom door, I froze

as I saw my uncle laying in the bath, I couldn't bare another go at being his wife! " I'm not good at being your wife uncle Phil, I think I'm not old enough, I would really like to go home now" uncle Phil didn't reply, he didn't move, I wandered if he had fell asleep in there. I walked closer to the bath tub to check if he was sleeping, his eyes were wide open and he looked cold, the radio was still plugged in but now it lay in the tub beside him. I'd never seen a dead body before but somehow I knew that's what I was looking at. I backed out of the bathroom and phoned home, Sammi answered, I remember saying he's dead Sammie, and then I felt Emily squeeze me, at least I think I did, I hugged her tightly and hung up the phone "was this you Emily" but Emily didn't answer. I wasn't sad that uncle Phil had died, I didn't really understand what death was, I just knew in my heart that me and Sammi were safe now, I whispered to Emily "thankyou", and I'm not sure what happened next.

Chapter 5

I watched as Carol tidied around in the kitchen, happily singing along to the radio, this seemed like it could be a good home for me, Sammi and of course Emily. I heard Brian's voice shouting in the distance, his sister Brittany came running into the kitchen crying, Brian had punched her in the arm because he couldn't get his own way, how cruel to hurt your sister like that I thought to myself. Carol told Brian off and took away his tv privileges for the day. Brian got really cross and started screaming at carol ,telling her he's 13 now and she can't tell him what to do. Carol followed Brian to his room and confiscated some of his belongings until he had calmed down and accepted his original punishment of no tv. Brittany sat next to me at the table, *"my brothers a jerk, I'm going to teach him a lesson someday"* I just looked at her, I understood her pain.

Tommy Tribble was a boy in my school, he was a year above me, in the playground everyday he would tease me, ever since I stopped talking. Tommy would make fun of Emily too, he said I was too old to have a doll all the time. One time he grabbed Emily from me and threw her into the nursery playground, he said that's where she belonged. I climbed over the small fence to retrieve her, she had sand in her hair and all over her dress, I was so upset that Tommy would hurt Emily like this. I climbed back over the small fence and caught my knee on a sharp bit of wood, I cried as my blood dripped onto the floor, I clutched Emily tightly and ran to the girls bathroom. Scrunched up by the side of the toilet I cried as I told Emily how sorry I was that Tommy had hurt her, I told her he wasn't a very nice boy at all. As I gazed at the small pool of blood growing on the floor I stopped crying, I looked Emily straight in the face and again repeated " Emily, Tommy is not a very nice boy, in fact he's a very bad boy", I didn't know if Emily had listened , I'm not sure I knew what I was wishing onto Tommy, I just knew that bad people deserved to be punished.

I took hold of Brittany's hand in an attempt to let her know that I was there for her, she looked at me peeking through her long hair which she wore half covering her face, I wasn't sure how old she was, Brian was definitely older, but not by that much. "We`re home" Ed shouted from the front door" , I ran to see Sammi, I hugged into her like I hadn't seen her for a year, *"its ok luce, I'm back now, your safe"*. I studied her face for a moment, was that the beginning of a smile appearing in the corners of her mouth? Maybe Sammi was right last night when she told me today would be a better day, if my big sister was almost smiling again then it certainly was a better day.

"Right everyone, who's up for a trip to the park?" Ed said excitedly. I smiled at the thought of playing on the swings like a regular normal child, I thought about leaving Emily at the house but I feared that may upset her, she likes the swings too after all. We all walked the 10 minute walk to the park, it was quite busy, there was lots of other families there enjoying their day.

Sammi and I headed to the swings, we had to wait our turn but it didn't take too long. I hopped onto the next available swing and Sammi started to push me, I went so high it was like I was flying, I felt like a bird soaring through the sky, untouchable, I felt I could do anything, I let go of the swing and outstretched my arms like a golden eagle, beautiful and breath taking, before I realised what was happening I felt my body slam into the ground, Sammi was rushing around me checking if I was ok and apologising for pushing me to high, I didn't blame her, I liked flying high, then I saw the blood dripping from my knee, it was just like that day at school.

I woke up in the school toilets, I couldn't remember going to sleep, how long have I been here? I straightened myself up and cleaned the dry blood off my knee. I hurried back to my classroom worried I was going to get into trouble for being late. As I approached the door I noticed through the window that everyone was still outside, playtime mustn't be over, I thought to myself, I wouldn't get in trouble now. I ran outside and saw there was something going on by the gates, then I noticed the ambulance, I ran over to Sammi to find out what happened. "it's that boy Tommy Tribble, he's had a bad accident, he must have been climbing over the nursery fence and he slipped, a piece of the broken wood went right through his neck". I took a step back, how awful, although he deserved to have an accident, he was a horrid boy, but not an accident that bad, I looked down at Emily, I remembered waking up in the bathroom, what had Emily been doing whilst I slept, why did I sleep? None of it made any sense, I hugged Emily, if she had anything to do with it I know it's just because she was trying to protect me.

I snapped out of my self-taught trance, Sammi was crying saying how sorry she was, said she didn't mean to hurt me, it was an accident, *"you understand that don't you luce, I'd never hurt you on purpose, I'm not a bad person"* I hugged Sammi tight letting her know I didn't blame her, she seemed so scared, was she scared of me? I would never wish her any harm, she's the only person who has ever looked out for me, it hurt me to think I scared her. I clung onto Emily and whispered over and over in my head that Sammi is a good person and no harm will come to her, I found myself fearful of Emily's protectiveness, but I felt for sure she would never hurt my sister, the only person I had left in this world that loved me, Sammi would be fine, I would never let anyone hurt her.

Chapter 6

Back at the Bowlers house Carol took out a first aid kit from underneath the sink, it was cute little green box with a white cross on it, she took out some cotton wool and asked Sammi to pass her a bowl of warm water. As she dabbed the wet cotton ball across my knee I felt numb, it didn't hurt anymore, nothing seemed to hurt anymore, not like it should.

Sat in the reception area at school waiting for the nurse to be free I listened to a conversation that was going on between the receptionist and a teacher "poor Tommy, the wood when clean through his neck, I've been telling the head for months now that we needed to do something about that fence" I cringed listening, looking down at Emily she looked quite pleased with herself, happy in her thoughts, she certainly seemed too calm to have done anything wrong, maybe I'm being silly and Tommy's accident was exactly just that, an accident.

"Lucy Lampson" the nurse called, I sat on the chair whilst she cleaned up my knee, "aren't you brave Lucy, you know I've had older kids in here crying at me whilst I clean their cuts, you must be made of strong stuff", I didn't respond, I was too busy thinking about Tommy Trimble, he was always very mean to me, and to a lot of other kids my age, once I saw him spit water at a little boy in nursery! That was definitely mean, he deserved a punishment, but was the punishment he was now suffering a bit extreme? He was after all still a child himself, The head walked into the nurses office," I just thought I'd let you know that Tommy's mother just rang, she said he's going to be okay, he's going down for a fairly simple operation and after a couple of weeks rest he should be back to normal". The head teacher, Mrs Smith seemed very pleased with this news, her smile filled her face, I felt this was an unusual look for her, she had always seemed so mean looking, she barely spoke to any of the kids other than to chastise us, a smile felt out of place, up until now I didn't think she could smile, id thought maybe someone had stolen it away from her when she was a little girl too, " did you hear that Lucy, Tommy's going to be just fine" I studied the nurses face as she awaited my response, she seemed expectant, I remained emotionless, lost in my thoughts, do we really want Tommy back at school being his normal self. I think the nurse felt uneasy around me, she had the same look in her eyes that my dad always had, she told me I was good to go, as I stood outside her office for a moment gathering my thoughts I heard the head and the nurse whispering, I strained to listen without it appearing obvious, "Tommy said it wasn't an accident, he thinks someone pushed him" I froze for a minute not sure how to react, I clutched onto Emily tight as I could and considered the awful truth that was no longer my imagination, I ran back to class quick as I could, I wanted to pretend the day had never happened.

Carol pulled out an assortment of plasters for me to choose from, I picked a pretty pink one, as she stuck it onto my knee I notice Emily had a little blood spot on her hand, I held out Emily's hand to show Carol that Emily may need a plaster too, Carol smiled sweetly, her face was kind, I barely even noticed the hairy mole staring straight at me, she took a wet cotton ball and attempted to wash away Emily's pretend wound, *" it's not coming off very easily Lucy, I think this blood is older than today"* I stared at Emily for a minute, I wondered whose blood it could be if it wasn't fresh from today. Carol let me pick out a plaster for Emily, I chose a pink one to match mine, Emily liked that. Carol packed away the first aid kit and sent me off to play with Sammi in the garden.

The Bowlers back garden seemed massive in comparison to our little back yard back home, it was green, and clean, there was a swing set and a slide and a playhouse, Sammi joined Brittany on the swings, there was no room for me so I went to explore the playhouse. It was a cute little house with yellow walls and a red roof, it had a door and a window but not much else, I played house with Emily, it felt normal, I enjoyed normal, sometimes the gut wrenching knots and the worried thoughts became too much, so normal was nice, I peeked out of my little round window to check on Sammi, she was chatting and giggling with Brittany, she looked normal too. Maybe all the bad stuff was behind us now, maybe it was our turn to be perfectly normal and have a normal life. I glanced happily out of the window and looked at the clouds rushing by, I could make out a fluffy sheep with a hat on so I giggled to myself. Over in the distance I noticed a strange cloud, it was big and black and it looked quite scary, was it a cloud at all? It looked similar to the smoke from the night my mum died.

I woke up on the pavement outside our little terraced house in Salford, Sammi was tugging my arm and screaming at me to move, I heard a lot of background noise, people were shouting, there were flashing lights and a siren was blaring, before I could make sense of what was going on a big strong fireman scooped me up and took me down the street out of harm's way, his muffled voice was talking to me but I couldn't quite grasp what he was saying as he shined a torch in my eyes, there were muffled voices all around me and I felt a mask being put onto my face, after what felt like an hour but was merely a couple of minutes I started hearing and seeing things clearly, the smell of fire smoke stung my nose and my eyes were burning with tears that I couldn't control, I didn't understand, I knew I wasn't crying. I pulled my arms to my chest to hug Emily but fear set in when I realised Emily wasn't there, I sat up, my eyes searching, I could see now, I was in the back of an ambulance, through the open doors a fire lit up the night sky, smoke bellowing like big black rain clouds, I realised then that it was our little terraced house that was burning down, panic overtook me, where was Sammi? I pulled off my mask and tried to search around for her but I couldn't see her, my eyes stung again but this time I think it was from real tears, I mustered up the strength to let out a scream, one that could wake the dead, and then I felt my head fall back onto the bed defeated. " Its ok Luce, I'm here, and I have Emily, you're okay " Sammi came bursting onto the ambulance, we hugged and cried, I had never felt such relief, not even when I saw uncle Phil dead in the tub, this relief beat that hands down. We were taken to the local hospital to be checked over properly, we didn't speak, we just sat in silence, I clung to Emily and Sammi held onto my hand so tight I thought my circulation was going to stop. "I think the police want to ask you some questions girls, I will let them know you're ready for them" , Sammi looked at me worriedly, " what happened luce? Do you know? Did you tell Emily about what mum did?" I stared at her blankly, had no recollection of anything, all's I knew is that I woke up on the street.

Chapter 7

Lying in the bath tub after tea I thought about the day we had just had, for the first time in a long time I felt like a normal child, I felt happy with the day, I mean sure id fell off the swing and hurt my knee but that was a normal thing too. Sammi was smiling and giggling again and it appeared she found a new friend in Brittany, I felt a little bit jealous and occasionally I would let a thought creep into my head out of fear of losing Sammi but id quickly shut it down, after all I had Emily so it's only fair that Sammi has a friend too. I would usually tell Emily all of my thoughts and fears but id tried keeping a few to myself lately just in case, and I certainly wasn't going to tell her about my silly jealousy stuff.

Mums funeral is tomorrow, I wasn't looking forward to it, it had barely been a week since she died but it felt a lot longer. Grownups say a funeral is a last chance to say goodbye, I feel like I already did that the night she died, not that I fully remembered the fire, but if I thought about it, and I mean really thought about it, I could remember more.

"Brian stop it!" Brittany's scream broke my thoughts up, I wondered what that mean boy was doing now. I heard a loud smack followed by crying, I hurried out of my bath to see what was going on. In my bedroom Brittany was curled up with her hand nursing her reddened face. Sammi was furious, "that Brian's a bloody bully! He needs teaching a lesson" I looked at Sammi longing for her to tell me why she was so upset, she looked at me and saw the worried look on my face, *" it's okay Luce, he's just being a stupid boy that's all, you wait here whilst we go talk to Carol and Ed".* I felt excluded, but I knew she was only trying to protect me as she always did. I stood on the landing looking down the

stairs trying to hear what was being said but it was no use. A bedroom door creaked open and Michael appeared, he was a very quiet boy, sometimes id forget he even lived there. *"your sister and Brit ok?"* I just shrugged, it was the most he had ever said to me, did he know I didn't speak? *"I saw what happened, but I couldn't say nothing, Brit tried saying something and she got a slap across the face for it, if he can do that to his own sister he would do much worse to me!"* what else did he see I wandered, I squoze Emily tight as I could feel my anger rising, what did Brittany try and stop him from doing? Did he hurt my Sammi? I stared angrily at Michael, how could he, a boy just stand there and watch another boy bully girls, I felt Emily's grip getting tighter, or was it mine? I took a few deep breaths and calmed my temper, I studied Michael, he didn't have much about him, a girl half his age could probably beat him up, some people are just more cowardly than others, I had to accept that in life. My dad was a coward, scared of his little girls imagination and running off without saying goodbye! My mum was a coward too! I found that just before she died. Michael moved closer to me to whisper, he didn't want Brian to hear him. *"they were playing a game and Brian went too far, he pinned Sammi down and tried to kiss her, she freaked out, screaming and kicking, Brian laughed and made fun of her calling her a baby, when Brit tried to make him leave her alone he slapped her across the face, he's trouble that one, definitely gonna end up in prison when he's older!".* I ran into my room, I could feel my anger growing bigger and bigger, but then Sammi walked in the room, she saw me trying to control myself, she sat by my side and held me tight *" it's okay Luce, we told Carol and Ed everything, they're going to deal with him the right way Luce, okay, its nothing for you to be worrying about"* she whispered to Emily, *"it's nothing for you to worry about either Em".*

Lying in bed later that night I was listening to the wind blowing outside, it sounded vicious and made me glad I was inside nice and cosy. Sammi had been asleep for a while now, she breaths differently when she's sleeping, smooth and deep, tonight though her breathing kept changing, this is why I was still awake, I could tell she was having bad dreams, I wandered if it was about Brian, or maybe mum? But then I realised it was the worst kind of nightmare *" no uncle Phil please"* she was talking in her sleep, she hadn't done that since just after dad left. Why now was she having nightmares about uncle Phil, he's dead, he can't hurt us anymore, Bloody Brian, he pinned her down and tried to kiss her! Had his actions made her remember the awful things uncle Phil did to her? I didn't know exactly what uncle Phil had done to Sammi, but she was going round every weekend for a few months, I was certain he done a lot more than what he had chance to do to me, Sammi had never wanted to speak about it, and I, well I hadn't uttered a word since the day I saw him laying dead in the tub. The doctors say it was shock at finding him like that, they think I will speak when I'm ready, I'm not in shock no more, not sure I ever was, I'm just always scared in case I say anything to get Emily in trouble, I couldn't bear to lose her, or if they think I'm bonkers and put me in the local nut house, they most probably wouldn't let Emily come with me anyway so I'd lose her either way, I could never let that happen. Sammi started crying in her sleep, she was so upset, I climbed onto the top bunk to comfort her, her sleep calmed down as I stroked her head, I hated uncle Phil for doing this to her, and right now, at this particular moment I hated Brian too, I hugged Emily tightly, "Brian's not nice Emily, he's hurt my sister, he's hurt his sister, he hurts everyone, he's a bad person" I was so angry, I don't think I meant to tell Emily that much, but right now I didn't care, I fell asleep cuddled up to Sammi, for once I was being her protector.

Chapter 8

As the police talked to us about the fire I stared at Emily, Sammi told the police lady I hadn't spoken in months since I found uncle Phil's body in the tub, the police lady looked at me sympathetically, her eyes urging me to speak, I could feel them burning into me, I continued to stare at Emily " was it you Emily?" I whispered in my mind, the policeman had a booming voice, he was a large man, he seemed to think everything had a reason, there's a reason the sky is blue, there's a reason I found uncle Phil's body, there's a reason I didn't speak and there's a reason our mother is dead! Yes there is a reason for all that, but not one you would ever understand! "the fire brigade say your mum must of fell asleep with a lit cigarette in her hand, it dropped into the side of the chair and a blaze engulfed the room quick as a flash, did any of you hear her screaming? Coughing? Any sign that she was still alive before you left the house? What woke you up? Why were there no batteries in your smoke alarm? I've got a lot of questions girls, I need some answer" he looked like an angry man, like a vicious dog digging for his bone, "Sammi?" I looked at Sammi and felt bad that this would fall onto her shoulders because didn't want to speak" , "Lucy woke me up, she was coughing and shaking me, there was smoke coming from under the bedroom door, we knew to stay low in a fire as the fire brigade came to our school last week and told us lots of things, they said how important it was that we had working smoke alarms, I made mum check them and they worked fine, I don't know what happened to the batteries, they were there last week, it makes no sense, mum drinks a lot at night time since dad left, its our job to check she doesn't fall asleep with lit cigarettes, I did that last night, I took the cigarette from her hand and put it in the ash tray with water like I always did, I opened the small window in the living room to get rid of the smoky smell so it wouldn't smell to bad in the morning and then I left the living room door open for that reason too and I went to bed" I studied the policeman's face, I think he believed her, he had no reason not to, she was being completely truthful, and I remembered the fire brigade coming to our school last week, it was fun, we got to sit in the fire truck, I had gone home and told Emily everything id learned, especially the part about smoke detectors being so important. I remembered smelling the smoke and waking Sammi, clambering down the stairs and out the front door, I remembered seeing the living room door shut and thinking it was unusual, I had wondered at the time if our mum was in there, Sammi was shouting for her constantly, id had to keep tugging at her so we could get out safely and then hitting the fresh air it all went blank. "anything you want to add young lady?" the big policeman was glaring at me and Emily, I shook my head, "dead uncle, mum just died, I hear a boy at your school had a bad accident as well recently" I nodded, "you seem to be around a lot of accidents don't you", "sir that's enough, she's a child, you can't interrogate her this way, this is upsetting enough I'm sure", the police woman looked a lot friendlier than he did, if I was ever to speak my truths, I would choose her, not him! Sammi hugged me tightly to protect me, I don't think she ever realised I was protecting her too.

Chapter 9

The morning sunlight blared through the window waking me from my slumber, I felt like I had slept like a rock, I stretched my arms out dramatically and let out a very satisfying yawn, today was going to be a good day, but then I remembered it was mums funeral today, maybe I had slept too late and missed it? I glanced at the wall clock, a big round clock with a white face and pink and silver trim, it fit in perfectly with the colour scheme of the room, it was 10:15, mums funeral wasn't until noon. I stood on the side of my bed and looked for Sammi, she must have already gone for breakfast. I jumped off the side of the bed and ran down for breakfast.

I walked into the kitchen and Sammi was sat talking to Brittany who had clearly been crying. *"Morning love, you ready for breakfast?"*, Carol was stood holding a plate full of bacon butties, I could smell the bacon grease in the air, it made my stomach rumble loudly, *" I will take that as a yes then"* Carol smiled. I sat down next to Sammi and tucked into my butty, curious as to why Brittany was so upset, what had that horrible brother of hers done now? "morning Luce" Sammi gave me a quick hug then took Brittany's hand and they went up to her room. Carol sat beside me looking worried, I could sense something wasn't right, *" I'm really sorry sweetheart but I'm not going to be able to come to your mums funeral with you today"* she must of seen the look on my face, *" I want to come and support you both I really do, but there was an accident last night"*, she paused for a minute, I could tell she was fighting back tears, I wondered what had happened to make her so upset, *" Brain fell down the stairs in the night, he must of lost his footing or something, we don't even know what time it happened, Brittany found him lying there unconscious this morning, he's in the hospital and there doing some tests on him because he can't remember anything, he's broke his leg too, poor love, so you see Eds had to go up to the hospital to be with him and I will need to be here to look after the others, you won't be alone though, your social worker Amanda is going with you"*. I stared at carol barely able to take in everything she just said, suddenly I didn't feel very hungry anymore, I looked down at Emily and wondered what to think. *"come on poppet, you need to go and get ready, don't you worry, I'm sure Brian will be just fine"*.

I sat alone in my room consumed by my thoughts, was this my fault? I held Emily out in front of me whilst I searched her face for answers, *did you do it Em?* I was really mad last night when I told her them things, I didn't mean for Brian to get hurt, I never meant for anyone to get hurt, well maybe uncle Phil but never another kid. Emily didn't answer me, she never did, if she can't even communicate with me is she really capable of doing these terrible things? Or am I just going slowly mad in thinking this?, Sammi came into the room, *"you ok luce?, I take it you heard about Brian"* I could feel Sammi's eyes darting between me and Emily, *"lucy, did you tell Emily about what Brian did? You know it wasn't even that bad, I just over reacted, there was no need for him to be hurt the way he is"*, I looked up at Sammi with tears in my eyes, I just didn't know what was real anymore, Sammi wrapped her arms around me and pulled me close *"its ok Luce, I'm here, I will always be here for you"*.

Amanda gripped hold of mine and Sammi's hands as the funeral car pulled up. Her hand was warm, she had a caring touch that made me feel safe. I sat in between her and Sammi on the way to the funeral, I had never been to a funeral before, wasn't sure what to expect. Sammi looked so sad, I rested my head on her shoulder to show her I cared but she didn't acknowledge me, she was too lost in thought.

There wasn't a lot of people at the funeral, it was a small service, we didn't have any family left now that mum and uncle Phil were gone, well my dad was somewhere but no one knows where. The 2 police officers from the hospital were there, I wondered if they just wanted to make sure we were all ok, maybe they knew we didn't have anyone else. The vicar was a funny looking chap, to be honest he looked as though he should be dead, his skin was pasty white and the wrinkles hid his features, he had a few liver spots on his face and hands and white wispy strands of hair sitting on top of his head as if the wind forgot to take them. When he spoke his voice was creaky and I couldn't make out everything he was saying, I did hear him say that our mum was a doting mother to her 2 girls and how sad we would be now she had gone, Sammi started to cry, I squoze her hand tightly, she must remember things differently to me, I remembered mum just sitting there all night losing herself in a bottle of vodka, I remember the cleaning always falling onto our shoulders, that we were forced into it but even me and Sammi didn't want to live in squalor . I remembered the nights we shared a piece of toast for our tea because mum had spent the last of the benefit money on vodka and not even given us a second thought. I don't remember this person the vicar was describing, I thought for a minute we may be at the wrong funeral! The vicar asked if anyone wanted to share their memories of her, Sammi looked scared and so much smaller than she was as she stood upfront next to the ageing vicar, *"I remember a summers day, august last year, mum took us to the funfair, we had the best day, it was like we didn't have a care in the world, we went on all the rides and got candy floss, Lucy laughed so hard after one of the rides that her drink came out of her nose!, and then mum treated us to a chippy tea on the way home , it really was the best day"* I had forgotten all about that, I smiled whilst Sammi was telling the story, memories flooding back to me like a tidal wave as I remembered happier times id blocked out, I realised then that I had always let the sadder memories shade over them. Sammie's happiness at reliving the memory turned to sadness as she continued, *"It wasn't until later that night when I heard mum crying that I realised what a day of happiness for us had cost her, she had been so desperate to give us a day that she felt we deserved that she had pawned her mums ring, it was the only thing she had left of her mum who died when she was little, it had always meant so much to her yet she gave it up just to make me and Lucy happy! That's the mum I remember"*, Sammi wiped her eyes and sniffed back the snot as she came back to sit next to me, I never knew about nannas ring, I didn't believe mum had ever cared enough about us to do anything so un selfish., I felt a tear roll down my cheek as other happy memories came back to me, a day at the beach, a picnic tea in the garden, cuddling up on the sofa watching tv on a rainy day, all things id buried long ago. Walking out of the church I grabbed hold of Sammi's hand but she pulled it away from me, she had never done that before, maybe she was just to upset for herself right now, she was allowed to be, I just held onto Emily tighter and took Amanda's hand instead. The police officers were waiting near the funeral car, they told Amanda they wanted to speak to her so we had to wait in the car. I strained to hear what they were saying but it was no use, I sighed and looked at Sammi, *" you know there suspicious don't you"* I stared at her blankly, *" they don't understand why all these accidents keep happening, and to be honest Luce neither do I!"* her tone was different, less caring, I felt like she was speaking to a stranger, I hugged Emily harder as the tears started to prick my eyes. *"I'm sorry Luce, but too much bad stuff is happening, I know its not really your fault but I,,"* she paused for a minute, reading my face, her tone became softer, more like the Sammi I knew, *"I just wish id never got you that doll!"* , how could she say that, she knew what Emily had meant to me, to us, she was our protector! I tugged my eyes angrily away from her gaze, *" the police know something isn't right Luce, I don't think they trust us?, and I don't think I trust Emily!, you know I found her on the floor outside the closed living room door that night don't you?, why was she there? She only ever went anywhere with you? Why would she be sat next to the living room door whilst our mum was burning to death? I should of bloody left her there to burn too"* Sammi burst out crying uncontrollably, I never knew any of that, I never knew where Emily was that night, id fell asleep cuddling her as I did every night since the day Sammi gave her to me, my mind went off on a tangent of everything bad that had happened since I got her, that's when it all started, that's when bad people got punished, but mum? Why would mum need that kind of punishment? Just then Amanda got in the car and comforted

Sammi, that was my job but Sammi didn't want me right now, we headed back to the Bowlers house in silence.

Chapter 10

Sammi had avoided me for a whole day since the funeral, it was the following morning as I lay in bed listening to the rain and lost in my thoughts that she finally spoke to me, *"I'm sorry Luce, I've been horrid to you and I never meant to be, I've just been so upset, I miss mum terribly and sometimes it's like you don't even care that she's gone, I'm sure you never wanted anything bad to happen to her though, I know she screamed at you that night, I heard it all the way upstairs but you never told me why? What did you do to make her so mad luce? Was it something you told Emily about?".* I cast my mind back to that night, it was the first time id even tried to remember what had happened, had I blocked it out for a reason?.

We were meant to be in bed by now, it was past bed time but mum was already halfway through a bottle of vodka. Sammi and I had been working so hard on finishing a jigsaw puzzle, it had 500 pieces, it was a picture of kittens playing, Sammi had promised when we finished it that we could glue it to some cardboard and put it up on the wall like a proper picture, I felt it would make our room look a lot better. Sammie yawned and climbed into bed but I just wanted to do a bit more because we were so close to finishing it. Our room was small with single beds on either side, the curtain rail was hanging off a bit causing the curtains to droop over. There was a big old fashioned wardrobe that I'm sure must of belonged to our great great grandmother or something and then we had a toy chest but most of the toys were too babyish for us now, a picture of kittens would certainly make our room look nicer, especially if we hung it over the damp patch. It used to be a very nice room, back when dad was here, he had been promising us for ages that he was going to decorate it just how we wanted it, I guess he forgot about that when he left us. I was so excited as I put the last piece of the puzzle in place, I couldn't show Sammi though because she was sleeping now so I decided I was going to surprise her in the morning, she's going to be so happy, especially if I get the glue and cardboard ready. I crept downstairs , mum looked like she had passed out already, Sammi had done her jobs for the night, taken the fag away from her and opened the window, I went through to the kitchen and started rummaging through the draws and in the cupboard under the sink but I couldn't find the glue anywhere, I was sure it would be there. I remembered mum moaning about ripping a letter the other day that she needed, maybe she used the glue to fix it. I was quiet as a mouse walking back into the living room and across to the sideboard, we were never allowed to go through the things in the sideboard cupboard, mum had always told us that's where she keeps her private stuff, things that have nothing to do with us, up until now I'd always kept my word and never even thought about going in it, but I really needed the glue. I felt guilty as I moved things around, still half trying to keep my promise by not looking, I must of nudged a pile of letters as one floated out and onto the floor, I shot a look over at my mum to see if she had woke but she remained the same. I carefully picked the letter up and went to put it back but I glanced at the writing, I noticed it said, "dear little sis", my mum only had the one sibling, uncle Phil, curiosity got the better of me so I started reading it.

Dear little sis

I hope you're doing ok & I hope you enjoyed the vodka I sent back with Sammi last weekend. As per our agreement I've enclosed the £50 for Sammi's weekend stay. I was wondering if you had given any more thought to what we talked about the other day. I really do feel it's time for Lucy to come stay now and earn this money, Sammi is getting a bit old and starting with attitude and trying to deny me what I want! If this refusal gets worse I'm going to start feeling like I'm raping the girl! I fear what may come out of her mouth. If you want the money to keep coming then I expect to see lucy stood there this weekend waiting for me with a smile on her face.

Love your big bro

I couldn't believe what I was reading, I stared in shock! Mum knew? All this time she knew what he was doing to Sammi and then she sent me to be ruined too! Before I could process what I was reading mum snatched the letter out of my hand and began screaming louder than I'd ever heard her scream before! I ran upstairs quick as I could and jumped into my bed and hid under the covers, "what's going on Luce? What's wrong with mum?" Sammi said in a sleepy voice, I stayed hid firmly under my blankets. How could she do this to us? She's meant to love us! Did the money mean more to her than we did? Anger surged in my belly, I gripped onto Emily, his words going around in my head, Sammi refusing, feels like rape! How far did he go? Was it really worth £50 ,to traumatise a child in this way, "she's just as bad as him if not worse" I whispered to Emily, how could she do this to us?, I cried to Emily for ages before I eventually fell asleep. I don't know how long I slept for but I woke up coughing, struggling to breath, then I noticed the smoke coming underneath the door, I panicked and ran over to Sammi, trying to cover my mouth, I was pushing and pulling her to wake up, " Luce, what's going on, what's happening? Oh my goodness, there's a fire", Sammi joined me in coughing, she kept screaming for our mum, I didn't care about mum! I cared about us getting out of there, Sammi grabbed a t shirt off the floor and pressed it to my mouth" you need to keep this here, try not to get too much smoke in your lungs, come on Luce we need to get out of here, keep low, move quick and don't let go of my hand okay", I nodded in agreement, it was so scary, our little house seemed like a mansion as we made our way down the stairs, they went on forever!, at the bottom near the living room door I saw Emily, the smoke was burning my eyes so I couldn't be sure but I swear there were some batteries on the floor beside her! Sammi scooped her up and we made it outside, the fresh air hit me, I took in a deep breath of the cool night air and then collapsed onto the floor happy we had got out alive.

Snapping myself back to reality I realised Sammi had climbed into bed with me, *"I guess I will never know what happened that night Luce, but I know whatever it was, it wasn't your fault, I'm just not so sure about Emily"* she gave me a long hug, "come on Luce let's get ready, the Bowlers are taking us swimming today, that should be fun right?", swimming sounded fun, I think we needed something to take our minds off things, but now I remembered what our mum done, I don't care that she's dead, I don't care that we had a few good memories because this bad one I now had would overshadow any amount of good ones forever. I hugged Emily, my protector, *"thank you for always being there Em"*. I kissed her forehead and got ready for a fun day swimming.

Chapter 11

The local swimming baths was busier than I thought it would be. Sammi and Brittany held hands and jumped in the deep end together. I wasn't a very confident swimmer yet, id only had a few lessons before school let out for the summer holidays. I decided id just sit and watch for a short while instead until I felt ready go in. The pool looked similar to the one id had my lessons in, it was just a basic rectangular pool with a smaller baby pool of to the side, I think all the council pools looked the same. There was one difference I noticed, in between the changing rooms and the pool there was a little stream of water you had to walk through, presumably to clean your feet, the one here was in clear view of everyone in the pool, in the swimming baths I used to go too it was more secluded, hidden behind a wall. I didn't really like my swimming lessons with the whole class, I was never allowed to take Emily with me, I had to leave her in the changing rooms.

It was swimming day at school and everyone was happy and excited, everyone except me! Id only had 3 swimming lessons before this and I knew the teasing was going to start all over again. We all lined up ready to climb onto the mini bus that took us every week and just like clock work Janey Jones bumped into me on purpose and set about accusing me of bumping her. Janey would taunt me constantly on the bus every week since swimming started. I didn't know what I had ever done wrong to Janey Jones or why she felt the need to pick on me, but somehow she always managed to have everyone laughing at me by the end of the journey. I always tried my best to ignore her, I would sit clutching Emily and just look out of the window until we arrived. Once we got into the changing rooms Janey's taunting got worse this time, she snatched Emily out of my hands and threw her to Lisa Bowden! They were both laughing as I was trying to get her back, I told them Emily wouldn't be happy with them and the whole room of girls burst out laughing at me! "just give her doll back Janey before she cries" Lisa said, "fine, here you go cry baby" Lisa threw Emily straight into the foot wash stream and burst out laughing. They all proceeded to walk threw the foot wash and to the pool but Janey made sure she stomped on Emily's head along the way. I rushed to get Emily out of the water, picking her up and squeezing her tight I told her how sorry I was that I hadn't been able to protect her. "That Janey Jones is an evil cow" I didn't usually say curse words, not even in my head, but I was so upset for Emily, what if she hurt her, what if she tore her pretty pink polka dot dress! I was so angry I told Emily to do whatever she wanted to that nasty girl!

The teacher, Mrs Greyson, came into the changing rooms to see what was taking so long, I couldn't even tell her what I was so upset about, she asked if I wanted to write it down but I shook my head, I started getting my clothes back on over the top of my still dry swimsuit. "what about your swimming lesson?" I looked at Mrs Greyson and shook my head, she could see how upset I was and even though she didn't know why, she agreed I could go and sit in the waiting area and read instead.

As I sat by the edge of the pool I giggled at Sammi and Brittany splashing each other, they were having so much fun that I considered joining in but they were heading to the deep end and I certainly wasn't confident enough for that. Michael come racing past me and cannon balled into the pool, we all burst out laughing, looking down I realised Emily had got wet, I frantically tried to dry her off, "it's okay Emily, nobody meant to wet you, it was an accident" I was so scared she would think it was deliberate like last time.

Sat in the waiting area reading I felt my eyes getting tired, I must of dozed off for a few minutes because next thing I knew there screaming and a lot of commotion coming from the changing rooms. I looked round for Emily but she wasn't there, I ran to the changing rooms and Mrs Greyson was stood holding her by the leg, as I got closer I noticed the foot wash stream was flowing red, Mrs Greyson grabbed my shoulder in an attempt to stop me from seeing but it was too late, lay face down in the water was Janey Jones, she was surrounded by blood which looked like it was coming from a large gash in her head, her eyes were open, she had the same death look that uncle Phil had. Mrs Greyson pulled me right away from it all so the paramedics could get by, she lead me out to entrance where all the other kids stood wrapped in towels, nobody could get to their clothes in the changing room because of what happened. Mrs Greyson passed Emily to me "Lucy, why was your doll left by the foot wash stream?" I looked up at her and shrugged, I really didn't know why Emily was there, she was in the waiting room with me earlier. I looked at Emily willing her to tell me what she had done, she never spoke, I hugged her tightly, If she had done anything it was my fault for telling her she could do what she wanted! Maybe this accident was actually my fault.

Carol broke my thoughts as she wrapped a towel around Emily to dry her off, I smiled at her, she really was a nice person, *" why don't you go have a splash around for 10 minutes, we will be going soon, I'll look after Emily for you, I promise I'll keep her safe"*, she smiled sweetly, I knew she was sincere so I took the steps into the pool and grabbed a yellow floaty for safety and off I went to have a bit of fun, shaking off them memories that haunted my mind.

We got back to the Bowlers house in time for tea, Ed had made us all fish fingers, chips and mushy peas, I had a big dollop of ketchup on the side of my plate, I liked ketchup with everything, Sammi laughed as the bottle made a fart sound. there was a knock on the door so Ed went to answer it. He came back into the kitchen followed by the 2 police officers. *"Sammi, Lucy, these police officers just want to talk to you, shall we go into the other room?"* , my stomach filled with dread as I clutched Emily to my chest, Sammi took my hand and squoze it tightly, was she as scared as I was?

We sat in the living room quietly waiting for the policeman to say something, it was the horrible mean man and the nice lady that spoke to us last time. The house seemed the quietest it had ever been, I could hear the clock ticking, it was a large black clock that took over the wall above the fire place, I thought it looked out of place but it was rather nice. *"how you both doing?"* the lady officer asked, Sammi told her we were doing okay considering. The police man butt in, *" we came to your mums funeral, you seemed to handle it okay Lucy"*, I looked at him, he had a wedding ring on, I wondered what his wife must look like, is he mean to her?, I just shrugged my shoulders. *"so the fire brigade have finished there investigation into the fire, it appears your mum fell asleep with a cigarette, I thought you said you had put it out Sammi?"* , *"I did!"*, Sammi exclaimed, *"I done everything I always did, maybe she woke up again and lit another one?"* He looked at her sternly *" Hmm maybe that's possible"*, *" It appears someone had taken the batteries out of the smoke alarm too, we found them on the floor in the hallway!"* I squoze Sammi's hand tightly and hugged Emily into my chest, *"maybe they fell out "* Sammi said, *"no that's not possible Sammi, was there anyone else at your house that night? Maybe you heard your mum arguing with someone? I get the feeling you 2 aren't telling me everything"* Sammi and I shook our heads, *"right well I've got a bit more digging to do so I'm sure we will be in touch again soon!"* *"let me show you out officers, I think you have everything you need for now and these girls haven't finished their tea yet!"* Ed butted in pointing to the door. I felt very nervous at the thought of the police digging around, what if they figured it out? What would I do? I started crying and hugged Emily, *"its okay Luce, they're not going to find nothing okay"*, but even Sammi's words didn't comfort me, I needed a plan.

Chapter 12

It had been a couple of week since the police came, maybe they had given up now I thought. I hadn't slept properly in such a long time, always thinking of what the police may find, hating the thought of what might happen next. Sammi's birthday was today, I had to forget all my fears for now and concentrate on making sure Sammi had the best birthday ever. Sammi had been so distant with me just lately, I know its because of everything she thinks Emily's done, she told me I should get rid of her. I was upset that she wanted me to be without Emily, she may have done some terrible things but it was only to protect us! Why wouldn't Sammi understand that?.

Brian was coming home today as well, he would be on crutches though so we had to be extra careful, he best not bother my Sammi today , I thought to myself. Sammi come bursting through the door, *"happy birthday to me"* Sammi seemed happy, it was the first birthday for ages that she was getting a proper birthday! *" I'm so excited Luce, I'm allowed 2 friends over for a birthday sleep over, you can join in too Luce, just, Emily isn't invited, I don't even want her meeting my friends, so you can come but I think its best if Emily sleeps in the playhouse outside, okay?* I was glad she was happy and she had invited me to her sleep over but I felt sad for Emily, what would she think about having to sleep in the garden! I decided make the playhouse all nice and cosy for her, maybe she wouldn't mind that much.

"Welcome home Brian", everyone cheered as he hobbled through the door, I was glad he was ok, id just rather he stayed at the hospital a bit longer, what if Emily was still cross with him?. Brian barely said 2 words, he looked sad and scared, he didn't look like he wanted to be back at the house at all. Brittany helped him into the living room and everyone left them to chat, I was curious as to what he would say to her so I stood outside the door listening. *"I don't trust any of them Brit! I'm telling you to be careful, my memories coming back and I know someone pushed me that night! Its still hazy and I cant remember who it was but I'm sure its gonna come back to me, you just be careful Brit, that's all I'm saying"*. I ran away quickly before I got caught, does he really know? I wondered if he saw Emily push him that night? I wondered what I should do next.

The doorbell went, *"I'll get it"* shouted Sammi excitedly, she knew it would be her friends. She took the girls straight up to our bedroom, and called out for Brittany along the way. She didn't call out for me, she had already made it quite clear that I could only come if I abandoned Emily for the night.

 I took blankets and a pillow out into the playhouse and got Emily settled. *"I'm sorry Em, I don't think Sammi understands that you only do things to help us, she seems scared of you, doesn't want anything to ruin her perfect girls night!"* I assured Emily that she would be just fine in the play house, she had everything she needed and I would check on her in a little while, I no it seems silly, but I couldn't help thinking her face looked a little sad, maybe she didn't want to be left out, I know I wouldn't like it if Sammi didn't let me join in. I gave Emily a kiss on the forehead and went indoors to join my sister and her precious friends.

Up in our bedroom there were sleeping bags laid out on the floor, bowls ready for the bags of popcorn, and Ed had brought us a tv and video player in for the night. *"Come on Luce, we got you a facemask here, were going to pamper ourselves before we watch a movie"* Sammi helped me put my face mask on, we all looked rather silly sat there with green gloop all over our faces, it made me laugh out loud. Sammi's friend charlotte looked at me, *"what's so funny?, have you never done this before? Maybe your too young to join in Sammi's night!"* I looked at Sammi for support but she just laughed with charlotte, *"is there something wrong with your sister Sammi? Why doesn't she speak?"* asked her other friend Sonia, *"there's nothing wrong with her, she just choses not to speak, she's fine, aren't you Luce?"* I nodded. *"Lets play a game, how about spin the bottle?"* charlotte chirped, everyone seemed excited at the thought of it, I didn't know what it was, I decided to just pretend to know what I was doing so they wouldn't think I was too young. Sammi went first because she was the birthday girl, she gave the bottle a twist and it landed on Brittany, *"truth or dare Britt?"* Brittany thought for a moment then chose truth, Charlotte jumped in quickly *" is it true that someone in this house pushed your brother down the stairs?"* Brittany looked shocked at the question, *"I don't know"* she said, *"come on Britt, okay then is it true that Brian believes someone pushed him down the stairs?"* Brittany nodded her head, *"but Brian's always been clumsy and always had an over active imagination!"* the girls laughed, Sammi let out an awkward laugh and looked at me, I just put my head down to avoid eye contact. Brittany spun the bottle next, it landed on me, *"truth or dare Lucy?"*, I felt a surge of panic setting in, if I picked truth what would they ask? Would they see threw my lies?, I quickly made my mind up that dare was probably my best option, *"dare"*, I said uncertainly. Brittany began thinking of my dare, she was a nice girl (unlike her horrid brother) so I doubted it would be anything too bad, *" I dare you to.."* Charlotte jumped in again! *"speak"* she said in a loud voice, I just looked at her, her face all covered in the drying gloop, she looked like an evil witch now, I didn't like her very much, not a good friend for my Sammi, in fact I didn't like either of her friends, acting older than they were and trying to make Sammi behave that way too, *" come on Lucy! It's a dare, you have to do it!"* Charlotte exclaimed, *" I dare you too speak, its not an unreasonable dare at all, Sammi says you can speak, you just choose not too, so now I'm daring you to speak!,* tears welled up in my eyes, why was she being like this with me, why couldn't she just leave me alone, I didn't do anything to her ever! *" leave her alone Charlotte!"* Sammi stuck up for me at last! *"if she doesn't want to speak she doesn't have too okay!"* Charlotte reluctantly agreed and then added, *"I'm not being funny Sam, but your sisters weird, she gives me and Sonia the creeps, and she's far too young for the sleep over, cant she sleep somewhere else?"* Sammi looked at me for my reaction, I took my pillow and blanket and headed out of the room. Sammi came running after me," *I'm sorry Luce, its just for tonight okay?"* I sighed and gave her my angry look, *" look Luce, its just 1 night, don't give me that look, you get me all to yourself all the time, I just want one good night with my friends, don't ruin this for me, and don't you dare tell Emily!"* she spun around and headed back into our bedroom and shut the door, I could hear them all laughing, I felt the tears roll down my cheeks, I wasn't sure if I was sad or angry, but I knew I definitely didn't like Sammi's friends! And if I wanted to tell Emily I would!

I sat on the top of the stairs wondering where I should go now, would Carol let me sleep on the sofa? Or maybe I could sleep in the playhouse with Emily, the sound of a creaky door broke my thoughts, I looked around and saw Brian staring at me from his bedroom. Brian looked sad, nervous, confused and maybe even scared, he had a whole bucket load of emotions coming from his face, I felt bad for a minute that he looked this way. *"aww did they kick the weird little baby out of the room"* Brian teased, I turned away in an effort to ignore him but he continued, *" I know that you or that stupid sister of yours pushed me ya know!, I cant prove it yet, but when my memory comes back properly I'm gonna make you pay, I'm gonna tell that copper everything, he's been asking me loads of questions you know, I bet he thinks you or your sister did this, and god knows what else"* he slammed his door and it made me jump. I hoped he would never get his memory back! And what's with that bloody nosey copper, why cant he just accept that accidents happen!.

Carol saw me sitting on the stairs with my pillow and blankets, *"oh poor love, have the big kids kicked you out?" never mind, how about we have our own movie night eh?"* ! I looked up at her and nodded sadly, she truly was a nice person.

I snuggled under my blanket on the big comfy sofa whilst Carol made us popcorn, id chose the movie ready, a nightmare on elm street, I hoped she would let me watch it, id seen it before when Sammi and I had a movie night with mum once, Sammi was scared all the way through but not me, mum had laughed at how I didn't even flinch, she joked I must have the devils blood in me, I never understood what she meant, I just knew I liked the film.

I could hear raised voices in the kitchen, Ed was shouting at Carol, I heard him mention bank statement, I think he was cross that she had been spending too much money, Carol was trying to shout back in more of a hushed voice, reminding him there were children in the house, Id never heard any of them shout before, it didn't seem right, this was meant to be a nice home for us all to live in happily, I walked towards the shouting, I felt I needed to get to Emily, she would always make me feel better when I was scared, and there shouting was certainly scaring me! *"why are you up? Get to bed!"* Ed saw me coming, I froze on the spot, *"leave her alone Ed, she's having a camp out in the living room"*, Ed threw his glass at the wall and it smashed everywhere, *"ED!!"* Carol screamed, Ed walked away back to his office room and carol was trying her best not to cry, *" I'm sorry love, eds not usually like this, he's just really stressed at the moment"*, I took Carols hand to let her know I cared, *"and another thing"* Ed came bursting back into the kitchen shouting, I ran out the back door and down the garden till I reached the play house, I climbed under the blanket with Emily holding her tight, *"I'm sorry Emily, I should never have left you out here all alone, everything's going wrong tonight, no ones being nice"*, I heard giggling coming from my open bedroom window, Sammi was in there clueless to what was going on downstairs, she had always been there for me but now that she's got cool new friends she doesn't care about me anymore, Eds turned into a scary angry monster that shouts and smashes things and makes people cry, and Carol says he's just stressed, yet he had that all to familiar smell about him, the smell uncle Phil had, the same smell my mum always had, stale smoke and alcohol. In an attempt to cover up mums short comings as a decent parent Sammi had once told me it was the alcohols fault, *"alcohol changes people luce, it makes them do and say things they never would"*, id accepted this once, but wondered, if that is what alcohol does to people then why would anyone ever choose to drink it? And if they drank it then any behaviour that occurs because of it should still be classed as their fault. The giggling got louder from the bedroom window, I wondered if they were laughing at me? Was Sammi joining in?, Ed was shouting in the kitchen still, I could hear everything as if it was the noise from a jumbo jet hovering above my head, images raced through my mind of mum and uncle Phil, I felt dizzy as uncontrollable tears streamed down my face dripping onto Emily's head and then, everything went black.

When I woke up I could hear Sammi screaming, I rubbed my eyes and realised my hands were wet, I didn't know what it was, it was too dark, I looked around for Emily but I couldn't find her and then Sammi screamed again, she was shouting my name. I ran back into the house not knowing what was going on, it was so quiet, Ed an Carol weren't in the kitchen anymore, I looked at the little clock sat on the window ledge in the kitchen, it was past midnight. I stayed very quiet as I walked through the house, it was dark but I didn't want to put any lights on in case I woke anyone up and got into trouble for sleeping outside. It seemed like every stair in the house was against me that night, creaking and cracking, moaning with every step I took as if I was as heavy as a giant. I finally reached the top. I slowly opened our bedroom door, I hadn't heard Sammi since, maybe I imagined it, I didn't want to wake her or them horrible girls up and ruin Sammi's night for her. As the door slowly swung open I could see Sammi's shadow sat on the floor, the moonlight was peeking through the curtains and shining straight on her, then I heard her sobs. *"what did you do Lucy? What did you do?"* she cried over and over again, I didn't know what she meant, Sammi stood up and put the light on, as I glanced around the room I didn't notice the pretty pink and blue décor anymore, the warm cosy room that had been our sanctuary didn't exist now, the big fancy clock on the wall was ticking louder than ever, Sammi began shaking me, looking for an *answer " I told you not to tell Emily, I told you!"* , there was blood everywhere, it was splattered up the walls, all over the clock and on our beds, laying on the floor were 3 girls, I knew it was Brittany, Charlotte and Sonia but they wasn't recognisable, there faces and bodies had cuts all over, it reminded me of a scene from a horror film, *"look at yourself Luce, look at Emily!"* Sammi kept screaming at me so I put my hands up to my eyes which were squeezed shut in a childish attempt to hide from it all, they were still wet, as I opened my eyes I could see they had blood all over them, I had blood on my pyjamas too, I looked across the room and saw Emily sat in the corner, she had that same happy content look on her face, but she was covered in blood, and there was a large kitchen knife next to her.

I fell to the floor hugging Brittany, she didn't deserve this, she had never done anything wrong to me! *" I don't know how were going to explain this Luce!, that coppers not going to believe Emily did it! No one's going to believe us!, we need to run Luce, pack a bag quickly, we need to get out of here before anyone sees what happened"* I nodded in agreement and in shock I threw some clothes into a bag and grabbed Emily, *"No!"* Sammi shouted, *"Emily's not coming Lucy"* I looked down at Emily , she wouldn't want to be left behind, *" look Lucy, I love you, your my little sister and I will always protect you, we don't need Emily's protection, she goes way too far Luce, I don't trust her one bit, its just you and me against the world from now on okay?"* I loved Emily so much, but I knew that Sammi was right, and Sammi would always be my first choice because I loved her the most, I hugged Emily and gave her a kiss on the head then I placed her back on the floor next to the knife, *"good girl Luce, let's go"*.

Sammi closed the bedroom door behind us and we went downstairs as quietly as we could so as not to wake anyone. Sammie stopped next to the office door, *"maybe there's some cash in here, were going to need money if were running away forever"* Sammie opened the office door and we headed over to the desk, rummaging through their private draws felt wrong, I didn't like it one bit, *"Found some, lets go"* Sammi whispered, as we turned to leave Sammi froze, "Shh, Eds asleep on the sofa", fear set in, what if he woke and caught us, what if he was still in an angry mood? What would he say about the terrible things that had happened that night?, *"come on Luce"* Sammi took my hand and began pulling me towards the door, I couldn't take my eyes off Ed just in case he woke up, as we got closer I noticed a glass on the floor at the side of his fallen arm, he must of drunk himself into a coma like mum used to, as I looked deep through the darkness I noticed something glinting in the moonlight, maybe his reading glasses I thought, but forcing my eyes to accept the darkness I realised what I was looking at, I pulled Sammi's arm and just stared at Ed, "what is it Luce? We don't have time for this!", Sammi let out an inward gasp and her hand flew up to her mouth to stop a scream from escaping. Ed wasn't sleeping, he wasn't in a drunken coma, he was another victim of Emily's wrath!, there was a silver letter opener sticking out of his eye socket and his throat had been slashed. We ran as fast as we could, barely caring about being quiet anymore, I wondered if there was anyone left alive in the house, I couldn't understand why Emily would hurt them all so badly, they didn't all deserve to die.

Chapter 13

It felt like we had been running forever, my legs ached so bad and I was sure my heart was going to jump out of my chest any minute. Our pace slowed down to a speedy walk, *"we have to keep moving luce, at least for a bit longer, we can rest soon okay?"* , I carried on moving, Sammi was always right and always did what was best for us. The streets were eerily quiet and there was barely any cars on the usually busy road, it felt peaceful in a weird way, I liked the quiet sometimes, it gave me time to think and get things straight in my head, but tonight I didn't want to think, what would Carol say when she woke up in the morning to the massacre that had occurred in her house? Is Carol even alive? She must be, she was always so kind, never done me or Sammi any harm, but then again, neither did Brittany, Brian would be so upset when he realised his sister was dead, I liked the thought of him being upset but not at Brittany's expense, was he even still alive?, I shook my head to stop myself from thinking. Sammie pulled me into a bush as we heard sirens heading our way, they sped right past us, maybe they were on there way to the Bowlers house, I quivered at the thought of Emily being there on her own, she must be so scared.

It was getting early morning now, the sun was coming up, we were both so tired but Sammi kept pushing us,*" its not far now Luce, uncle Phil's house is just a couple of miles away"* I froze on the spot refusing to move, why was we going there? I didn't understand. *"Its okay Lucy, uncle Phil's dead remember, Emily took care of that didn't she! We just need somewhere to go so we can rest and come up with a plan okay?"* , that made sense I suppose, I really did want to rest and there was nothing to be scared of now uncle Phil's not there.

A paper shop was just opening up, I tugged at Sammi and pointed, *" okay, I'm hungry and thirsty too, you wait here though lucy, you cant go in the shop covered in blood",* I hid around the corner whilst Sammi went in, it took her a while and I wondered what she was doing, I crept over to the doorway to see if I could see her, she was just getting served. *"your awfully young to be out here alone this early missy"* the man behind the counter was questioning Sammi, I willed her to keep quiet, he glanced to the door and caught sight of me, *" is she with you? She looks even younger, and was that blood on her face? What's happened? Are you okay?",* Sammi said we were fine and it was fake blood from our game, she paid for the things and left with the man shouting after her. we ran as fast as we could to get away from there. *"Lucy I told you to stay out of sight, why do you never listen to me or do as your told anymore?"* Sammi was cross with me, I hugged her to let her know I was sorry, she sighed and took my hand and we were on our way again.

Chapter 14

Finally we made it to uncle Phil's house, there was a for sale sign in the garden but you could see nobody had been there for months. The street was starting to wake up so we hurried around the back, Sammi picked up a brick and smashed it through the glass window pane in the back door, we quickly got inside, shut the door and then both let out a sigh of relief.

The house still smelt the same, still smelt like uncle Phil, I found it more unbearable now than I ever had. All his furniture was still there, un touched and covered in dust and cobwebs, I giggled at the thought of uncle Phil hating how messy it was and knowing there was nothing he could do about it made me laugh harder. *"what's wrong with you?"* Sammi snapped, she sounded cross, *"what is there to giggle about Luce? Do you realise how bad everything is? Nothings ever going to be normal for us again and you're here giggling!"*, I hung my head, I know things are bad, I just don't see the point in being sad all the time, bad things happened, now there over, we can forget about them, but Sammi didn't see things like that, sometimes I think she likes to be sad. *"just get some sleep Lucy, we both need sleep and then we can come up with a plan okay?"*, I nodded in agreement, curled up on one side of the dusty sofa and closed my eyes, I had left space for Sammi but she sat in the chair instead. Is she blaming me for everything? She keeps getting cross with me for no good reason, I felt if anything I should be the one getting cross with her, none of this would of ever happened if it wasn't for her!. She gave me Emily to protect me and then gets cross when she does, It's her fault I had to go to uncle Phil's, It was her I was trying to make happy when I went down for the glue that night, it was her, her, her! every time something bad happened it was because of Sammi. My mind started over thinking angrily, how do I even know it was Emily doing these horrible things? Maybe it was easier for Sammi to accuse her! I knew I was being silly, I was just really angry with Sammi at the minute, she just needs to stop getting cross with me! I cried silently, I wondered how much longer Sammi would be there for me? Emily would of made me feel better, she would have cuddled me to sleep and made me feel safe! I just missed her so much and I blamed Sammi for making me leave her behind, everything just felt like Sammi's fault! I was so angry with her.

I remembered a time, not long after uncle Phil had died, because of my secret trauma I had stopped speaking, school had got the social services involved, my social worker had decided counselling might be the best option for me.

I was sat in a big comfortable chair in a very clean office, a thin lady sat opposite me jotting down in her pad, "so lucy, how have you been?" I shrugged, "you don't want to tell me?" I shrugged, " maybe you could show me" she passed me a small pack of cards that had different faces on each of them to

*express emotions, " which one best describes the way your feeling right now?",
I flicked through the cards, happy , sad, angry, hurt, guilty, they were all there, I
placed each card down, " my, that's a lot of emotions for a little girl to have" ,
why do you feel this way? I shrugged. "hhmm, let's try something different
shall we", she passed me a piece of paper and some crayons, "how about you
try and draw me a picture to describe why you don't feel like speaking", that
sounded like a really hard thing for me to do, how am I suppose to draw the
fact that I'm scared of what will come out of my mouth?. The lady stood up and
left the room saying she would give me a few minutes and return shortly with
juice and biscuits. I thought hard of a way to express myself in a drawing, I
closed my eyes and picked up a crayon and just drew. When the lady came
back into the room she gasped a little bit shocked at my drawing, I opened my
eyes to see and my page was covered in black angry scribbles, darkness and
confusion was the best I could come up with. I only had a few meetings with
her but because I wouldn't speak and barely participated in our sessions she
concluded I was bottling a lot of emotion up but unless I opened up there was
nothing she could do for me, I never saw her again. My social worker Amanda
would visit once a week, always trying to get me to speak, and each time left a
little less hopeful than the time before, I assumed she would get fed up of me
eventually, but she kept coming back, and was always polite to Emily too.*

I was awoken by Sammi screaming for someone to stop! I wondered what was
going on, when I opened my eyes and focussed I could see I was sat on top of
her! What was I doing? *"please don't Luce, I love you, I'm your sister!"* I didn't
know what she was on about, what did she want me to stop? Sammi was
crying uncontrollably and then the door flew open, *"Lucy, put it down"* put
what down what's going on? The angry police man stood there with his arms
stretched out, there was 2 more officers surrounding him, *"you don't want to
do this Lucy, you need help! Let us help you, just put it down before you really
hurt Sammi"* I suddenly realised I had something in my hands held above my
head, it was a large knife from the kitchen, Sammi was crying and she had stab
marks in her hands and cuts on her face. *"Sammi"* I said out loud in a scared
shaky voice as I started lowering the knife to the floor trying my best not to
hurt her anymore, Sammie pulled her defensive hands away from her face and
looked at me, *"Luce, is that you again?"* I nodded and burst out crying, I dint
know what was going on, the police man lifted me off Sammi and took me to
his car whilst the others stayed to tend her wounds.

In the back of the car I couldn't understand what was happening, I remembered nothing of the attack, why would I ever want to hurt Sammi? I know I went to sleep angry with her but I loved her the most in the world. I thought maybe Emily was there, maybe she found where we were and she made me do it. Did Emily ever do anything? I wasn't so sure anymore.

When I got to the police station Amanda was there waiting for me, I ran to her crying and broken, *" oh Lucy, I don't know what's been happening to you but I'm going to make sure you get the help you need okay",* I looked up at her through my sobs and saw that she was crying too.

Amanda and the angry policeman took me to what they said was a hospital, I was hoping they were taking me to see Sammi but this wasn't the usual hospital, I was shown into a small white room with a very basic look about it. The walls were plain and there was a small chest of draws in one corner and a single bed in another and a washroom to the side. It didn't feel right, any room id ever had id shared with Sammi, where was her bed? There was a small window too but I couldn't see what was outside right now because it was too dark by the time we got here. *"You get a goodnight sleep and I will see you tomorrow okay Luce"* I ran after Amanda as she left but I was stopped at the door by a man in a white coat. He shut the door and left me alone, I tried the door handle but I was locked in, is this prison? I lay on my bed alone and scared, I just wished I had Emily right now.

I don't feel like I slept at all that night, I didn't know what was happening and I was worried about Sammi, I didn't even know if she was alive! I`d thought about it all night long and it made no sense, I knew I would never try and hurt Sammi but Emily may have been angry with her for making me leave her behind, I was certain that Emily was behind this somehow.

"good morning Lucy, I've brought you some breakfast" a short stumpy man came into my room with a tray, he had very little hair, especially in the middle, his face was old looking and stubbly but he smiled as I tried to see the name badge hanging from his neck. *" I'm doctor Bakin, I will leave you to eat your breakfast and then were going to have a chat in my office , okay?"* he left the room locking the door behind him. I was starving so I tucked into my cereal and toast like id not eaten in months. After breakfast I went to the bathroom to wash and do my teeth, looking in the mirror I could see I still had blood on my face, I scrubbed and scrubbed, I wasn't even sure who's blood it was. I put on a fresh set of clothes that had been left for me, just some lose fitting

trousers and a t shirt, then I waited. I felt so much better now id eaten and got clean.

In his office, doctor Bakin just kept talking and talking, *"do you remember what happened yesterday Lucy? What about your foster parents house, do you remember anything from there?"* I had decided being mute again was my only option, he would soon finish with his questions and then I could just go back to Sammi and we could live at uncle Phil's house forever.

I was at the hospital for about a week, every day was the same, doctor Bakin would ask me the same questions over and over and I would just stare blankly at the wall, he would have to give up eventually.

"You have a visitor today Lucy" doctor Bakin announced at our next meeting, I looked around but no one was there, was this a trick to make me speak? *"your social worker Amanda is here and she has brought your sister Sammi with her, Sammi is a little nervous though so I just wanted to prepare you okay?"*, I nodded eagerly, it was the most communication he had got out of me all week, but why would Sammi be nervous of me? Surely she would know it was Emily that made me hurt her, it wasn't really me.

Amanda walked into the office holding onto Sammi's hand, Sammi looked scared, she seemed weaker looking than I remembered, pasty white face and dark circles under her eyes like she hadn't slept for a year. She had stiches in three different places on her face and her hands were bandaged up, how could Emily do this to you I thought as I ran to hug her. Sammi backed away from me and moved in closer to Amanda. *"Sammi's feeling a little nervous Lucy, just give her a bit of space, lets sit at the table eh!"* Sammi could see the hurt and confused look on my face, *"do you remember what you did Luce?"* she held her bandaged hands to her face, *"this was you Luce, not Emily, you did this, you did all the terrible thigs!"* she broke down crying and buried her head into Amanda! I shook my head in vigorous disagreement, how could she think that, she knows what Emily is like! *"you don't agree Lucy?"* doctor Bakin said questionably, I shook my head again! Sammi looked up at me, *"use your words Lucy, you said my name that night, I know you can speak if you want to, speak for me, help me to understand why you wanted to hurt me so bad?"* Sammi was crying uncontrollably, I could barely make out what she was saying in between the broken sobs, she jumped up and ran out of the room, abandoning me knowing I was upset too!. Amanda picked up a bag she had brought with her, she reached into it and pulled out Emily. I was so happy to see her I jumped out of my seat to grab her, I didn't even care that she had done so much bad stuff, I just knew a cuddle from her would make everything better, she would never abandon me like Sammi did.

Doctor Bakin looked at me, I could feel his stare judging me, probably wondering how I could love a murderous doll, I didn't care, he can think what he wants! *"Lucy, Sammi tells me that you think Emily is responsible for all the bad things that have happened to people, is this true?"* I glared at him! I wasn't about to say anything that would get Emily in trouble. *"she's just a doll Lucy, look at her, she didn't do anything wrong!"* I glanced down at lucy, her tatty hair needed redoing and her dress needed a wash, there were still blood stains on her arms and legs but she didn't care, she just sat there smiling the same as she always did. Doctor Bakin sighed, *"I was hoping I wouldn't have to go this far Lucy"* he took a large envelope out of his draw and began pulling out photos, the first was a photo of uncle Phil lay in the tub, he looked exactly the same as I found him that day. *"do you remember this Lucy? Did you push the radio into the bathtub? You were there that night wasn't you, your first sleep over with him?"* I just kept looking at Emily waiting for him to just stop talking. *"Sammi has been very brave and told us what your uncle had done to her every weekend, did he do something to you? Is that why you punished him Lucy?"* I didn't acknowledge his question, I didn't want to think about what uncle Phil had done to me or Sammi, shut up shut up shut up I just kept repeating in my head. *"Do you remember this person Lucy?"* It was a picture of Tommy Tribble, he had stitches on his neck from where they had removed the broken wood, *"the police spoke to a few of the children at your school, they seemed to think Tommy teased you a lot about Emily, is this true? Tommy doesn't talk very well since his accident but he did manage to tell the police that someone pushed him onto that broken fence, do you remember that Lucy?"* I hugged Emily harder. *"how about Janey Jones, she was in your swimming group wasn't she, had an awful accident that resulted in her dying, you were there that day too, in fact her friends say she had spent all morning teasing you and picking on Emily to upset you, is that correct?"* I could hear in his voice he was beginning to lose patience with me, I think these photos were upsetting him a lot more than they were upsetting me. He threw out another one, a smiling photo of Brian, how dare he look happy after upsetting my Sammi the way he did, I brushed my hand quickly across the table sweeping all the photos onto the floor in temper, I didn't want to see these photos, I just wanted to get Sammi and get out of there! *"are these photos upsetting you Lucy? You don't look very saddened by them, you look more angry than sad, say something lucy!"*, I just focused on Emily, ignore him and he will go away eventually. Then in a last ditched attempt to make me talk, or make me remorseful he threw a whole bunch of photos on the table, I glanced at the nearest one, it was Carol, she was lay on the sofa with her throat slit open, I felt sad to see this, Carol had always been so nice to me, oh Emily why did you do this, why would you hurt carol? I made myself look at the rest of the photos, everyone was dead, even poor Michael who would never hurt a fly! The photo of Brian made me giggle, he had a tv smashed into his head, how silly I thought, what a silly way to die, *"how can you laugh Lucy? All these people are dead because of you, not your doll Emily, You!, you hurt people, you killed people it was all you Lucy not your silly doll"* Doctor Bakin seemed so cross, he snatched Emily out of my arms, his words piercing through my ears, it sounded like a high pitched dog whistle, it was driving me crazy and then, nothing, darkness, I could hear voices but I couldn't make out what they were saying, everything was black.

When I finally got enough energy to open my eyes again I realised I was back in my room, the door was locked and there was no sign of Emily. I sat on the edge of the bed wondering how I got here, I was in the doctors office a minute ago cuddling Emily, I felt woozy and sick so I had to lay back down, I closed my eyes and decided I just needed to sleep and when I woke it would all seem better.

It was early morning before I saw anybody again, I felt like I had slept forever. There was tray on top of the draws with a now cold meal on, I hadn't even heard anyone bring it in. But now a new doctor I hadn't seen was standing in my doorway with another man dressed in white, *"hello Lucy, I'm doctor Mitchel, I've come to take you to another hospital, one which will better suit your needs"*, I stared at him for a moment and wondered what he meant by `my needs`, and where was doctor Bakin? why wasn't he telling me what was going on? The two men each placed a hand on my shoulders and lead me out to the car. It was a black car, I'm not sure of the make, it certainly wasn't as nice as Amandas black BMW. As I sat in the back I noticed there was a barrier up between the front and back, I could still see and hear who was in the front but I couldn't touch them, I wondered if this was for my protection or theirs?

The drive was very long, I thought for sure we must be going to a different country. I closed my eyes for a moment, getting sleepy from the rocking motion of the car, the doctor and the driver must of thought I was asleep, *"how's doctor Bakin?"* the driver asked, *"I heard he had an accident?"* my ears pricked up. *" it was no accident Carl!"* doctor Mitchel exclaimed. He went on to tell him how I had attacked doctor Bakin in our last meeting, said I jumped unexpectedly over the table, grabbed his pen and lunged it into his eye! That didn't sound like something I would do at all! *"the girls social worker Amanda was there, she had to pull her off him and scream for help, it took another 2 people to get her under control so they could sedate her"* I couldn't believe what had happened, I didn't remember any of it. *"bloody hell doc, you sure were safe here?"* the driver let out a little giggle, *"were fine Carl, she's had a mild sedative, it will keep her calm until she's locked safely in her new room at the secure facility"*, and with that they turned the radio on and the conversation was over.

Maybe my new room will be nicer than the last, I hoped Emily would be sat on my bed waiting for me. I smiled at the thought of me, Sammi and Emily having girly sleep overs at our new home, its just the fresh start we need. I opened my eyes and glanced out the window, the trees were whooshing past so quickly they just looked like one big long bush, can't count these trees I thought to myself. I Looked up to the sky and saw the clouds looking down on us, I stared at them intensely until I could see images, I'm almost certain I saw Emily smiling down at me, I closed my eyes slowly no longer having the strength to fight the sedation, I used my last bit of strength to remind myself that everything will be better after a sleep, it always is, my Sammi says so.

In my dream state I remembered the night my dad left as if it was yesterday. I could hear him and mum arguing. Dad was telling mum that I needed help, "she's not normal, there's something not right in her brain, we need to take her to a doctor", mum snapped back at him, "there's nothing wrong with her, she's just got a wild imagination!" dad was pleading with mum to see sense. "what kind of wild imagination decides to kill a cat? She slashed that poor cat up so bad whilst he was still alive! She smiled whilst she did it!", Mum yelled back at him defending me, "she said she didn't even do it, she doesn't know what you're talking about", "I saw her with my own bloody eyes!" dad yelled back, "I'm going out, I can't cope with this, I need to calm down but I'm telling you now, first thing in the morning I'm taking her to the doctors whether you like it or not!", I ran out to dads car quickly so he didn't see that I had been eves dropping, he jumped into the car and drove, didn't even check the back seat. He drove for a long time, I knew where he was going, where he always went to think, a large lake at the other side of Manchester. As he got nearer to the lake he started punching the steering wheel, he was so angry. Did he know I was *there? I thought about all the things he had said to mum, how could he think such horrible things of me? He`s my dad, he`s meant to love me no matter what and now he wants to take me to a doctors when he knows there's nothing wrong with me, he knows I don't like doctors, I got so angry with him I picked up a large heavy tool which was lay on the floor in the back of his car, before I knew what was happening I hit him hard across the back of his head. The car spun out of control, dads head resting on the steering wheel with blood coming from it. Within seconds I noticed the car was filling with water, I scrambled as fast as I could to escape from the drowning car, it felt like forever and for a minute there I thought I was going to die. I eventually made it to the side of the lake, I lay on the grass panting, grasping for breath whilst watching the last bit of the car disappear into the water.*

I ran all the way home that night, I didn't even stop to rest. I took the fields as they were a shorter route, I knew this because dad took me and Sammi to the lake once but then he got drunk and passed out so we had to make our own way home, Sammi showed me this short cut. It was early morning when I got home, the sun was starting to come out, I quickly changed my pyjamas and climbed into bed, I was so exhausted I could of slept for a week.

The car went over a large bump waking me from my sleep, I thought about the dream I had just had. I considered for a moment if it was just a dream or in fact a reality? Things like that had seemed a bit confused lately, I wasn't sure what was real anymore. I shook the thought from my head, don't be silly Lucy, you didn't even have Emily then so you wouldn't of hurt anybody. I was happy with my explanation, I looked out the window, the car was going slower now, I could see the trees properly, all there greenery swaying in the late summer breeze. I started to count them as they flew past my window, it helped me to not think so much, I didn't like to think, its always better to just count the trees.

The End

Printed in Great Britain
by Amazon